Alice's Special Room

Alice's Special Room

BY DICK GACKENBACH

CLARION BOOKS · NEW YORK

Clarion Books
a Houghton Mifflin Company imprint
215 Park Avenue South, New York, NY 10003
© 1991 by Dick Gackenbach
All rights reserved.
For information about permission to reproduce
selections from this book, write to Permissions,
Houghton Mifflin Company, 2 Park Street, Boston, MA 02108.
Printed in Singapore.

Library of Congress Cataloging-in-Publication Data
Gackenbach, Dick.
Alice's special room / written and illustrated by Dick Gackenbach.
p.   cm.
Summary: Alice tells her mother about her special room, where she
can play with her cat who died, enjoy the warm beach in January, go
sledding on a hot summer day, and do anything she has already done
in the past.
ISBN 0-395-54433-5
[1. Memory—Fiction.   2. Mothers and daughters—Fiction.]
I. Title.
PZ7.G117A1   1991   [E]—dc20
90-42352   CIP   AC

TWP   10 9 8 7 6 5 4 3 2 1

Concentrated watercolors were used to create the full-color artwork. The type is 20 pt. Palatino.

"I have a very special room," Alice told her mother one day.

"Oh," replied her mother. "How special?"

"This morning I played there with Louie," Alice said.

"Your cat, Louie?" her mother asked.

"Yes," said Alice.

"But Louie died last summer," said her mother.

"We played together in my special room," Alice said. "Louie and I played with bells, balls and string, and paper bags just like we always did."

"What else is in that room?" her mother wanted to know.

"Well," Alice told her, "do you remember how cold it was in January?"

"I do," said her mother. "You were tired of the cold and snow by then."

"There was a warm place in my special room," said Alice. "I sat there in the sun. I sat by the water and played in the sand."

"A room like that," said her mother, "is a good place to be in January."

"My special room is a good place to be on a hot July day, too," said Alice. "I can find a cold and snowy corner where I can ride my sled."

"My!" said her mother. "You're lucky to have such a room."

"I know it," Alice agreed.

"Maybe you'll go in that room sometime when I need a little peace and quiet," her mother teased.

"Don't make fun of me," said Alice. "There really is a special room, but I'll bet you can't find it!"

"I'll bet I can!" said her mother. "Give me a clue. Is the room downstairs?"

"It could be," said Alice.

15

So Alice's mother looked in the pantry.
"There's nothing here," she said, "except
canned goods, noodles, and spaghetti.
Nothing special about that."

She looked in the den. "Nothing special
here, either."

Alice giggled. "You're not even close," she
told her mother.

Alice's mother looked in the living room. There was nothing special there. She looked in the dining room.

"It's just a plain old dining room," she said.

"You're not looking hard enough," Alice told her.

So Alice's mother went to look upstairs. She looked in the bedrooms. She even looked under the beds.

"Maybe the room is so tiny," she said, "that I'll find it down here."

Alice laughed. "Maybe you will," she said, "and maybe you won't."

Alice's mother looked in the bathrooms and behind the shower curtains.

"Nothing there," she said.

Then Alice's mother opened the door of every closet.

"Well, I guess I'm wrong again," she said.
"I was sure your special room was in a closet."
"Keep looking," said Alice.

Then Alice's mother went up to
the attic, where she hadn't been for
a long, long time.

"It must be up here," she said.
"The attic is the last room in
the house."

When they got to the attic,
Alice looked around at all
the old things her mother
had stored away.

"This is not my special
room," she told her mother,
"but you're very warm."

"I give up!" her mother said.

"I'll give you one last hint," Alice said. "In my special room I can only see people I've met before. I can only go places I've already been. And I can only do things I've already done."

Alice's mother smiled and hugged her daughter. "That special room is your memory!" she said.

"You've guessed it," said Alice. "Would you like to go there with me?"

"I would like to very much," her mother said. "You lead the way."

"Well-l-l," said Alice thoughtfully. "Do you remember when I was little and Grandpa gave me a kitten for my birthday?"

"I certainly do," said her mother. "Your grandpa loves kittens."

"Me, too," said Alice.

Then the two of them had a good time remembering a birthday party with Grandpa, and a cat named Louie.